HALLOWEEN IS COMING!

words by Cal Everett

pictures by Lenny Wen

sourcebooks
jabberwocky

Published by Sourcebooks Jabberwocky, an imprint of Sourcebooks Kids
P.O. Box 4410, Naperville, Illinois 60567–4410
(630) 961-3900
sourcebookskids.com

Library of Congress Cataloging-in-Publication Data is on file with the publisher.

Source of Production: 1010 Printing Asia Limited, North Point, Hong Kong, China
Date of Production: April 2021
Run Number: 5021013

Printed and bound in China.
OGP 10 9 8 7 6 5 4 3 2 1

For Mom and Dad, who taught me about the frights and fun of Halloween.
For my kids, Cory, Emily, and Cam who joyfully share my passion.
For my grandsons, Julian and Noah, who will carry the legacy to a new
generation, and for my wife, Wendy, who has tolerated my indulgence in
creepy, crawly, spooky, and scary stuff every October for forty-five years.
—CE

To my family.
—LW

Look around, you'll see the signs
Getting dark at dinner time

Leaves are falling on the lawn
Spiders spinning webs 'til dawn

Feel the chill, it's in the air
Hayrides at the autumn fair

Look around, the signs are clear
Halloween is getting near

Pumpkins at the farmers' market
Jack-o'-lantern when we carve it

Scarecrows lurking all about
Corn mazes to figure out

That time of year when we can play
on castles made from bales of hay

Look around, the signs are clear
Halloween is getting near

Mom buys candy at the store
Skeletons on your front door

Candy apples, sticky sweet
Practice shouting, "**trick-or-treat!**"

Marching in the school parade
in frightening costumes that we've made

Look around, the signs are clear
Halloween is getting near

Full moon peeking through the clouds
Streets are filled with costumed crowds

This special night when you can be anything you want to be

Cowboys, soldiers, witches, doctors,
ghosts and goblins, queens and rock stars

Wizards, astronauts, and farmers,
zombies, robots, knights in armor

Prince and princess, clown and mime,
Mummy, Wolfman, Frankenstein

Be anything, be what you want
There's always one more house to haunt

It's tricks, and treats, and frights, and fun,
and spooky things for everyone

Look around, the signs are clear

Halloween is finally

HERE!

HOCUS POCUS

TRICK OR TREAT!